JANOSCH

The Old Man and the Bear

TRANSLATED BY EDITE KROLL

Bradbury Press / New York

10 9 8 7 6 5 4 3 2 1

The text of this book is set in 14 pt. ITC Garamond Book Condensed.
Book design by Lynn Braswell

Library of Congress Cataloging-in-Publication Data / Janosch. The old man and the bear. Translation of: Der alte Mann und der Bär. Summary: One very cold winter, an old man who buys birds in the market so he can set them free is helped by a bear who, after the old man dies, takes over his good work.
[1. Kindness—Fiction]   I. Title.
PZ7.J24401   1987   [E]   86-28362

Along time ago, there was an old man who

lived close to our village.

He spent each summer gathering mushrooms and berries in our woods and working in our fields. We called
him Gregory and thought him a fool, for he saved what
little money he earned until winter.

Usually around Christmas, Gregory walked to the market, where a foreign merchant sold birds he had trapped to the villagers. There was no radio yet, so people kept caged birds to hear them sing.

"I don't need cages," said the old man, and he bought as many birds as he had money to pay for.

Gregory would hold a bird briefly in his hands, then set it free.

The bird man also thought Gregory a fool, but he didn't care as long as he got his money.

Whenever the bird man had a sick bird, Gregory bought it. He gently placed it in a small cage he pulled out from under his jacket. He would feed the sick bird through the winter, give it water to drink, and when it was well, he would set it free.

Years passed, and the old man grew older and weaker. He could no longer do much work in our village. One summer he gathered very few berries and mushrooms and wood for his stove, and when Christmastime came, he had very little savings. But since the bird man knew Gregory, he gave him a sickly, gray bird at half price. It was a finch.

"A worthless kind," said the bird man. "It doesn't sing, not even in summer."

Gregory tucked the little cage with the bird under his jacket and trudged off through the snow. But he didn't go home. He had used up all of his wood, he had no birdseed left, the water in his well was frozen solid, and the little gray bird was too weak to look after itself.

"We'll go to the bear," the old man said to the finch.

Soon, a fox fell in behind them, then two hares and two crows. By the time they reached the bear's den, Gregory could no longer feel the cold in his legs and he felt light enough to fly.

"Who is that man?" shouted the bear, since bears and people are not great friends.

"This is Gregory," said the fox. "I know him well."

"What does he want?" asked the bear.

"Only a little food for this bird," said the old man, who felt as if he were floating on air and as if his voice came from far away. "And water, please," he added. "Otherwise it will die."

"All right," rumbled the bear. He gave the finch water and food and it felt better.

The animals prepared a bed for the old man, who felt himself floating again . . . up to the stars and into a great white light, as if carried on wings.

The old man had joined the angels.

Another winter came and it was even colder than usual. Snowdrifts had almost closed off the bear's den, and he had run out of provisions. The summer before, the bear hadn't gathered enough honey, and the snows had come early, before the berries were ripe, before there were enough fallen leaves to make a warm bed.

At Christmastime the bear said to himself, "I'll go to the village. Maybe I'll find something to eat there."

And he stomped off through the snow.

The night was pitch black and the snow was deep. The bear hadn't eaten for a long time and he grew weaker and weaker. Soon he couldn't pull his legs out of the snow and he fell down. The village wasn't far, but the bear felt too weak to get there.

Then, a little bird arrived. It was the finch. It perched on the bear's neck and whispered in his ear:

"Can you carry me to the village, bear? I might get something to eat there. Otherwise I will die."

"Yes," said the bear. He pulled himself upright and carried the finch into our village.

They noticed a light in the village church, but the sexton
would not let them in.

"This is no place for bears and birds," he told them.
"The villagers might be frightened."

The bear lay down outside the church door and kept the bird warm in his paws. The bird sang to him. When the people came out of the church, the children called out:

"There's a bear, Mommy! We must feed him! Maybe he's an enchanted prince!"

But the parents said, "A prince! Ridiculous! Besides, there's plenty of time to feed it tomorrow."

But when they came back the next day, the bear and the bird were no longer there. An angel had carried them off to the stars.